T.J.
and
agsby

Granny
Rose

Mudpie

A
Furnace for
Castle
Thistlewart

Written and Illustrated by
Barbara Alexander

Oak Tree Publications, Inc.
San Diego, California

A FURNACE FOR CASTLE THISTLEWART is part of the Make Believe & Me series.

A FURNACE FOR CASTLE THISTLEWART text copyright © 1985 by Discovery, Inc.
Illustrations copyright © 1985 by Barbara Alexander.

First Edition.

Manufactured in the United States of America.

Creative supervisor and world-wide licensing through Howard Wexler, 300 East 40th
Street, New York, New York 10016.

Library of Congress Cataloging-in-Publication Data

Alexander, Barbara, 1940–
    A furnace for Castle Thistlewart.

    (Make believe & me)
    Summary: A homeless dragon finds shelter in the basement of a castle and provides
    heat for its inhabitants.
    |1. Dragons—Fiction. 2. Castles—Fiction| I. Title. II. Series.
PZ7.A3766Fu   1985 |E| 85-21384

ISBN   0-86679-018-7

1 2 3 4 5 6 7 8 9 88 87 86 85

For Gary and "Ponnie-Mo"
who played "Pur-tend" with me

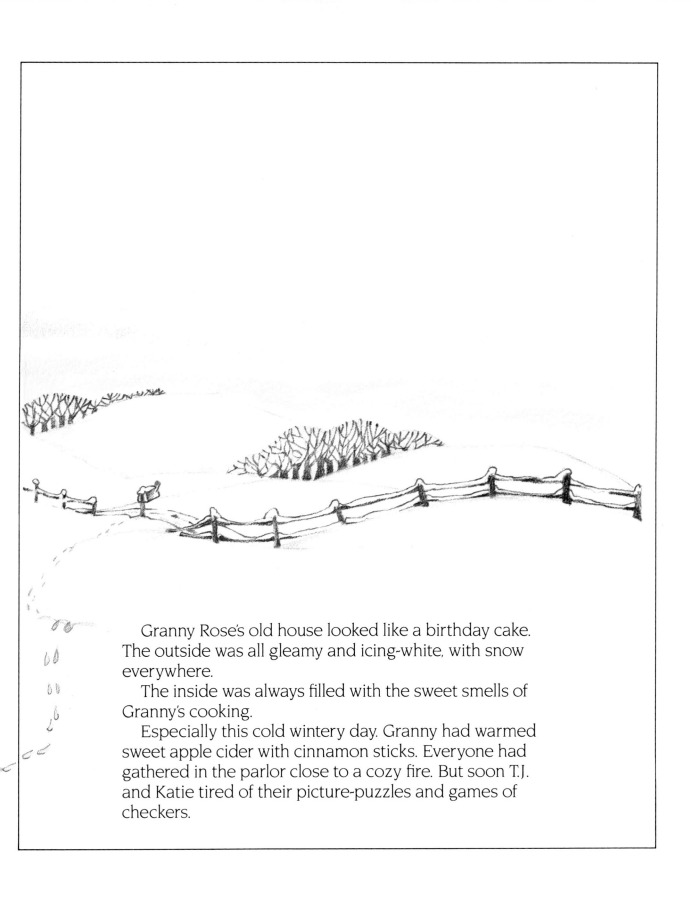

Granny Rose's old house looked like a birthday cake. The outside was all gleamy and icing-white, with snow everywhere.

The inside was always filled with the sweet smells of Granny's cooking.

Especially this cold wintery day. Granny had warmed sweet apple cider with cinnamon sticks. Everyone had gathered in the parlor close to a cozy fire. But soon T.J. and Katie tired of their picture-puzzles and games of checkers.

"T.J., let's go out and make a snowman," Katie said, looking out the window at the deep, fluffy snow.

"Let's build a beautiful snow castle instead," said T.J., putting on his heavy jacket and cap.

They built their snow castle in Granny's front yard . . . and as they rolled and packed and patted the snow, they began to play "make-believe." Make-believing was something Katie and T.J. did on certain special days, and today felt like one of those days . . . .

"My toes have never been this froze!" complained T.J.'s teddy bear, Ragsby. "If I'd known we were going to 'make-believe' ourselves into a 'fridgerator' I would have worn my boots and earmuffs."

"Me, too," moaned Cassandra, the cat. "I wish I had remembered my mittens!"

Mudpie, the dog, had brought Granny's big black umbrella. But it did little to keep the blowing snow off their heads.

"I think I see something up ahead!" T.J. spoke through chattering teeth.

"Let's hurry! If it's a house we can warm ourselves there!" Katie said.

As they came closer, they discovered that the shape was not a warm, friendly house at all, but something much larger. Far above them was the cold, dark tower of an enormous castle! In many places, the building stones had crumbled away, leaving walls no longer able to keep out the wind and snow. An old sign hung above the drawbridge:

CASTLE THISTLEWART
Visitors Welcome
Please Ring Yon Bell
......Signed H.R.M. King Fred

"Is this a 'Dracula' kind of place?" asked Ragsby in an "afraid" voice.

"It does look haunted!" whispered Katie, inching closer to T.J.

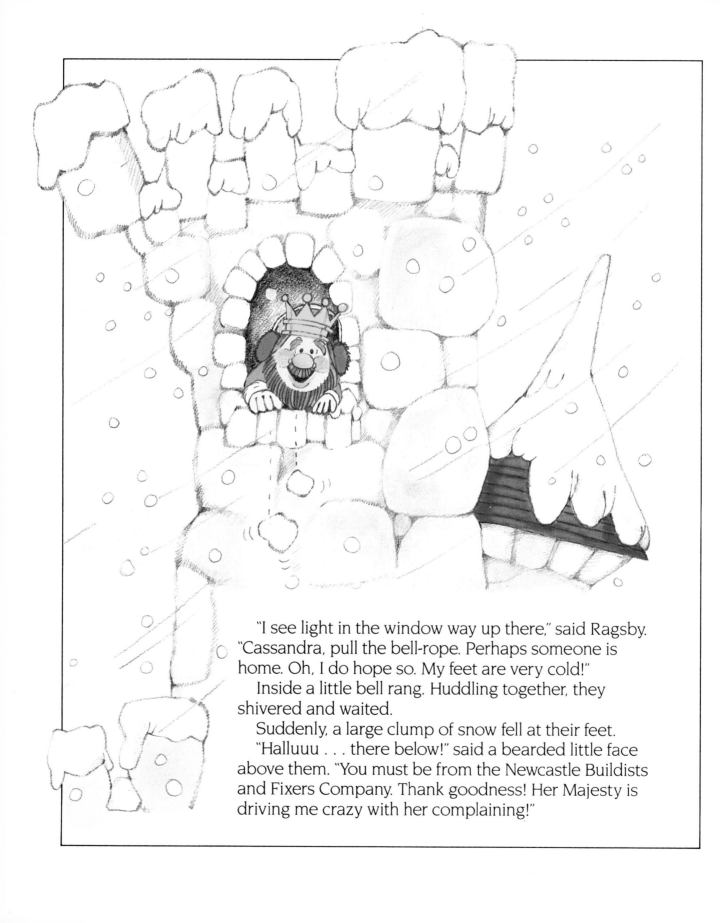

"I see light in the window way up there," said Ragsby. "Cassandra, pull the bell-rope. Perhaps someone is home. Oh, I do hope so. My feet are very cold!"

Inside a little bell rang. Huddling together, they shivered and waited.

Suddenly, a large clump of snow fell at their feet.

"Halluuu . . . there below!" said a bearded little face above them. "You must be from the Newcastle Buildists and Fixers Company. Thank goodness! Her Majesty is driving me crazy with her complaining!"

"Kind sir, may we please warm ourselves by your fire?" Katie asked politely.

Before she could finish, the bearded face said, "Wait there!" and popped back through the window.

In a blink, a door next to the drawbridge creaked open.

"Oh, do, do come in! I, Good King Fred, bid you to enter." The chubby little King bowed low.

"He talks funny," Ragsby whispered to T.J.

"Please go upstairs. The only warmth we have is from a small fireplace in the Queen's bedroom," King Fred explained.

The dizzy stairs went round and round. Breathlessly, they reached the top in time to hear a screechy voice saying, "Oh *hush*, Caruso! We are *not* amused."

The Royal Canary was whistling "Jingle Bells."

Annoyed, Queen Maude pulled her big fur coat tighter. Standing next to her, shivering noisily, was Sir Beans of Jelly, the King's favorite knight. The Royal Cook, Dolly stirred a small pot of soup in the fireplace.

"Fred, who *are* these people?" sniffed the Queen. "They don't look like the Newcastle Buildists and Fixers to me."

Katie and Cassandra stepped forward and curtsied.
"Your Majesty, maybe we can help," Katie said.

Queen Maude fell back in her chair, sobbing, "Nobody
can! I won't live like a bear anymore! I am going home to
my mother!"

"Wait!" the King yelled over her earsplitting boo-hoo's. "I'm about to proclaim something!"

"What's 'proclaim'?" Ragsby whispered. "Is he going to be sick?"

"I hereby order . . . beginning tomorrow . . . that great amounts of rocks and stones and wood be gathered . . . We shall build a *new* Castle Thistlewart! Now, let's have some soup."

For days, King Fred and Mudpie ran in and out, up and down. Thousands of castle pictures were drawn, and hundreds of lists were made.

Dolly cooked and cooked. Throughout the whole day, she kept a pot of chicken noodle soup and loaves of thick, crusty bread ready for the hungry workers. Queen Maude, Katie, and Cassandra made the new curtains. Every afternoon, they sat together, sipping cups of hot chocolate while they sewed and chattered.

Meanwhile, Sir Beans, T.J., and Ragsby went off in the snow looking for building rocks. Slowly, a pile of large rocks began to form in the castle courtyard.

It was late in the afternoon when the tired gatherers
came upon the *enormous rock* for the first time.

"Look there!" said Sir Beans, pointing. "That is the
biggest rock I have ever seen!"

They stopped their wagon and crept closer. For
several minutes, they just stared up at the big rock in
amazement.

Ragsby was the first to find his voice. "This is the most
specialest rock I have ever seen! Look at all the beautiful
colors!"

Rich greens and purples, lovely pinks
and blues glowed under the covering
blanket of snow.

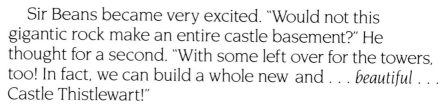

Sir Beans became very excited. "Would not this gigantic rock make an entire castle basement?" He thought for a second. "With some left over for the towers, too! In fact, we can build a whole new and . . . *beautiful* . . . Castle Thistlewart!"

That very night, the winter winds blew so warmly from the south that by morning, spring had come to Thistlewart. Everywhere the snow melted in splashy drips.

The old castle was filled with excitement. No one could talk of anything but the wonderful rock. After breakfast, strong ropes and ladders were found, and Sir Beans led them to the marvelous rock.

In daylight, with the snow almost gone, the enormous rock looked even larger. The colors shone brighter and more beautifully than the day before.

In no time, they tied their heavy ropes around the gigantic lump. When they had finished, Queen Maude yelled, "Heave-Ho" in her loudest voice, and the pulling began.

Oh, how they *pull-l-l-l-ed*! But nothing happened. So they *pull-l-l-l-ed* again. And again, nothing happened. Once more Maude bellowed, "Heave-Ho," and they yanked their mightiest *yank*, but the rock would not move at all!

"Perhaps it can be pried loose," said King Fred.

Sir Beans and T.J. found a heavy tree branch and put it against the edge of the huge rock.

To the point of collapse, they strained. The beautiful rock simply would not budge. There was nothing left to do but to leave without it. Sad and disappointed, they gathered up their ropes and turned to go.

Suddenly . . . the earth began to tremble! With a monsterous rumble and a thunderous roar, the rock began to *move*! A blast of fire erupted from the rock. Clouds of thick black smoke filled the sky. The huge lump gave a mighty shake and rose high into the air. It was not a rock at all—but a real-live, honest-to-goodness, fire-breathing *dragon* waking up!

Terrified people ran screaming in all directions. The dragon rubbed his sleepy eyes and, when he saw all those screaming, running people, he screamed, too.

When the smoke had cleared a little, Sir Beans crawled out from behind a tree.

"Sir Dragon, please excuse our rude behavior. We mistook you for a rock." His voice quivered with fright.

The dragon squinted into the clearing smoke. When he located the owner of the little voice, he lowered his mighty head. Gently, he touched Sir Beans with the end of his long, forked tongue. "Don't be afraid, brave little knight. My name is Heartburn. I won't hurt you! Dragons are like bears—we sleep all winter long . . . and wake again at the first sign of spring. This year the winter ice and snow came before I could find a cave to sleep in."

"Oh, pooh!" sobbed Queen Maude, forgetting to be afraid. "Now there is no beautiful big rock! And *no* beautiful new castle!"

The dragon looked at the unhappy faces below him and for a moment, he began to feel sad, too. Suddenly, he snorted and said, "I have an idea! Although I cannot *be* the rock for your new home, I am big and strong and can lift very heavy things. May I *help* you build your new castle?"

In a wink, the sad faces changed. Everybody laughed and cheered and hugged everybody else. On the way back to the old castle, they sang and chanted "Hip-Hip-Hurray" and "For He's a Jolly Good Fellow" until the blushing dragon begged them to stop.

For months and months, building sounds were heard in the Kingdom of Thistlewart. With Heartburn's help, a beautiful new Castle Thistlewart soon stood in place of the old one.

When the work was finished, the dragon came to them with tears in his eyes. "My good friends, I must leave you now. It is time for my winter sleep. This year, I must find a cave."

"Oh, please don't go!" Queen Maude was the first to burst into tears. "We have come to love you, Heartburn!"

"Wait!" the king yelled. "I'm about to proclaim something again! I hereby proclaim . . . beginning *now* . . . this fine dragon need never go away from us! Our castle basement shall be his home, and his fiery breath will warm our rooms all winter long. Heartburn, dear friend, you shall be a furnace for Castle Thistlewart!"

And so it *was*…happily ever after. The gentle dragon warmed the rooms of Castle Thistlewart with his blazing breath—and the hearts of his friends with his very special love.

Back in Granny Rose's front
yard, T.J. and Katie put the finishing
touches on their snow castle.

"I love it when we make-believe," said T.J.

"Me, too," said Katie, shivering.

"T.J.! Katie!" called Granny Rose from the house. "How
about some hot apple cider?"

"Here we come!" shouted T.J. and Katie.

"4"   "5"   "6"   and   the Grey one   Katie

cassandra